May your gift
always make room
for you in this world.

Thank you!

Cara M. McCall

September 18, 26

THESE HUGS ARE MY HUGS

BY DANA MCCALL
ILLUSTRATED BY IRFAN BUDI

It's the Holidays, and guess who we get to see? We get to see grandma, grandpa, aunts, uncles, and other family!

Ding, dong! **Ding, *dong!***

I wonder who is at the door!
More family, more presents, more,
more, more!

"Grandma, Grandpa!" we sang.

When our Grandparents come in, we give them the biggest hugs. Why, might you ask? Well, because THESE HUGS ARE OUR HUGS.

Knock, knock, knock!

I wonder who is at the door!
More candy, more presents, more,
more, more!

"Hi, auntie!" I exclaimed.

When my aunt comes in, she gives me a kiss. Then she hugs me real tight and calls me her little prince. It does not bother me; she always asks before she does it. I hug her back, because **THESE HUGS ARE MY HUGS.**

Ding, dong! *Ding,* **dong!**

I wonder who is at the door! More cousins, more presents, more, more!

"It's my uncle!" she yells.

When my uncle comes in, he gives me a high five. Up high, down low and he's usually too slow. We chuck and jab, and then I am on the go. My uncle is okay with this greeting, and I am too, *so...*

Knock, knock, **knock!**

I wonder who is at the door!
More candy, more presents, more, more, more!

"Hey Mom, I don't know who this is."

Now someone else is here, who I really don't know. She hands me a gift and tell me how much I have grown. I smile, reply "thank you," and then I shake her hand. "I am your mother's aunt, so that makes me your grand." "It's very nice to meet you." I say. I open the gift and then run off to play.

If you *wonder why*, I didn't give my hugs away, don't bother because I will simply say,

"THESE HUGS ARE MY HUGS."

Ding, dong! *Ding, dong!*

I wonder who is at the door. More family, more presents, more, more, more!

"Santa Claus!" I exclaimed. No, it couldn't be. Santa Claus is at my door, just to see me.

I kept telling my mom no,
but she kept pushing me to go
hug him.
I mean, if you really think about it,
there are way too many of them.
Santa here, Santa there, there and
there. Seriously, wherever we look
they are everywhere!

I watched the other kids go up, and he seemed okay.
He might be the real Santa, he just may!
I watch a little closer and decided on a hug. Why? Well, it was *really* my dad, and because

THESE HUGS ARE MY HUGS!

Made in the USA
Middletown, DE
07 June 2021